FIONA FRENCH

Hunt the Thimble

OXFORD   LONDON   MELBOURNE

OXFORD UNIVERSITY PRESS · 1978

Pieter, Anna and Edo
lived in a big tall house
by a canal in Amsterdam.

One cold winter's day
they played Hunt the Thimble
inside their house.

Pieter and Anna shut
their eyes tightly
and counted to ten.
Edo hid the thimble.
'Ready,' he called.

Pieter and Anna
ran into the kitchen
and looked under
the table and on top
of the cupboard.
But they didn't
find it.

'He's hidden it
somewhere too
difficult to find,'
said Anna.

They asked Kaatje the maid,
'Did you see where Edo hid the thimble?'
'No I didn't,' she replied.
'If he had come into this larder
I'd have chased him away.'

Anna went to see
Uncle Jan, a sea-captain
who was planning
a new voyage.
'Did Edo hide a thimble
here?' she asked.
'No,' he said firmly,
'Edo is not allowed
in here among my
valuable maps.'

Pieter went into the
music room.
His elder sister was
playing the harpsichord.

'Did Edo hide a thimble
in here?' he asked her.
But his sister was
    concentrating so hard
        she didn't hear him.

Then they asked
their father.
'Have you seen Edo?
He's hidden a thimble
somewhere difficult,
and we can't find it.'
'You had better ask your
mother about that,'
he replied.

They said to their mother, 'Edo has hidden the thimble somewhere so difficult that we can't find it.'

'Make him tell us where it is,' said Anna crossly. 'Edo,' called their mother, 'bring me back that thimble at once.'

But Edo didn't obey her.
He ran out of the house and
down the street.
'You can't catch me,
you'll never find the
thimble,' he cried.

Pieter and Anna ran after Edo,
chasing him through the streets
of Amsterdam.

They ran over the bridge by the Exchange, where the businessmen made their money. Pieter and Anna shouted to Edo, 'Wait till we catch you.'

But Edo didn't stop. He
collided with a man on the
bridge and nearly pushed
him into the icy canal.
Still he kept running,
shouting,
'You can't catch me!'

Edo ran through the
fish market and down to
the quay, where Kaatje was
buying fruit and vegetables.
He ran so fast that he
tripped over a chicken
in the street and . . .

. . . fell into
the middle
of the
vegetable
stall.

Everything went
flying into the air . . .
fish, lobsters,
cabbages, bread,
grapes, apples,
baskets, money,
and the little horse too.

Kaatje was extremely angry with Edo. Now look what you have done,' she said, 'you forget everything else when you start playing these silly games. Now you must clear up all these vegetables and put them back on the stall.'

Just at that moment, Anna saw the thimble.
'Here it is, Pieter. Look, the thimble!
It was on the little
horse all the time!'

But Kaatje was cross
with them as well.
'You are all just as
naughty as each other,'
she said, 'chasing your
brother right through
the town. Clear up
this mess or we
shall be late
home for
supper.'

'The next time we play Hunt the Thimble,'
said Anna to Pieter, 'it's my turn to hide it.'
They put everything back onto the stall,
so Kaatje wasn't angry with them for long.

'Perhaps you can have some supper after all,'
she said with a smile. But just in case
Edo ran away again she held
his hand tightly until they reached home.

1978

Oxford University Press, Walton Street, Oxford OX2 6DP

OXFORD LONDON GLASGOW NEW YORK TORONTO MELBOURNE WELLINGTON CAPE TOWN .
IBADAN NAIROBI DAR ES SALAAM KUALA LUMPUR SINGAPORE JAKARTA
HONG KONG TOKYO DELHI BOMBAY CALCUTTA MADRAS KARACHI

© Fiona French 1978

ISBN 0 19 279719 0

Printed in Great Britain by W. S. Cowell, Ltd., Ipswich